by Steven Banks   illustrated by Stephen DeStefano

Simon Spotlight/Nickelodeon
New York London Toronto Sydney Singapore

Based on the TV series The Adventures of Jimmy Neutron, Boy Genius™ as seen on Nickelodeon®

SIMON SPOTLIGHT
An imprint of Simon & Schuster Children's Publishing Division
1230 Avenue of the Americas, New York, New York 10020
Copyright © 2003 Viacom International Inc. All rights reserved. NICKELODEON,
The Adventures of Jimmy Neutron, Boy Genius, and all related titles, logos, and
characters are trademarks of Viacom International Inc. All rights reserved,
including the right of reproduction in whole or in part in any form.
SIMON SPOTLIGHT and colophon are registered trademarks of Simon & Schuster.
Manufactured in the United States of America
First Edition 10 9 8 7 6 5 4 3 2 1
ISBN 0-689-85465-X

Jimmy Neutron and his friend Carl were testing Jimmy's brand-new invention: the Robo Walker.

"This is your greatest invention ever!" said Carl.

Just then Jimmy's mother called out, "James Isaac Neutron, you come inside right now!"

Jimmy raced into the house, running up the stairs two steps at a time and into his room. Carl followed just in time to hear Jimmy's mother ask, "How many times have I told you to put away your pants?"

"Goddard!" Jimmy said, turning to his dog. "Access pants data!"
Goddard's screen popped on and flashed the number "54."

"I rest my case," Jimmy's mother said sternly. "You will not be going to the movies with your friends tomorrow night."

"But, Mom!" exclaimed Jimmy. "I gotta go!"

"You have to learn to pick up your pants first," she reminded him. "Pants just don't pick themselves up, you know."

After she had left his room, Jimmy thought about his mother's words. "Hey, that's it, Carl!" he said. "I can invent pants that will put themselves away! I'll just put nanochips inside."

"Are those the spicy ranch kind?" Carl asked.

"Not those kind of chips. Nanochips are microscopic supercomputers," Jimmy explained.

A while later Jimmy showed off his latest invention. "Mom, Dad, I now present Smart Pants!" he announced proudly. Everyone watched as his pants jumped toward the hanger and hung themselves up.

"Nice job, son!" Jimmy's father exclaimed.

Jimmy grinned. "I think this deserves the reward of going to the movies."

"Well, your pants did get put away," his mother agreed. "All right, you can go."

That night as Jimmy slept, a strange blue light began to shine in his closet. His pants were glowing!

The next day at school Jimmy's pants began to move on their own!

"Neutron, you big show off!" Cindy said. "You have to make everybody look at you, Mr. Big Science-Smart Guy!"

"I'm not doing it!" cried Jimmy. "I put nanochips in my pants so they'd put themselves away—but they seem to be getting smarter!"

Jimmy's pants began to vibrate and send out long tendrils to Cindy's, Sheen's, and Carl's pants. Their pants began to glow, making the kids jump and dance all around the playground.

"Neutron, you've got five seconds to tell me what's going on!" Cindy demanded. She began to limbo uncontrollably.

"My pants are controlling your pants!" cried Jimmy. "They're alive!"

Jimmy thought quickly. "I can fix this," he said. "I'll simply remove the nanochip from my pants."

But it was too late. Jimmy's pants had already peeled off him and were now running down the street! Carl, Sheen, and Cindy started to laugh. But a few seconds later their own pants peeled off and followed Jimmy's pants.

"Carl, Sheen, to my lab immediately!" Jimmy shouted.

In the lab the three boys tried to figure out where the pants were headed.

"I think my pants are going to try to get more pants under their control," said Jimmy. "My Eye-in-the-Sky Satellite will show where they are."

"Oh, no, they're going into the House of Blue Pants!" Sheen shouted. "There are a million pairs in there!"

"If my pants infect all the others, they could take over the world!" said Jimmy.

HOUSE OF BLUE PANTS

"We've got to stop our pants," Jimmy said as they climbed into the Hover Car.

"How?" asked Carl worriedly.

"Easy," replied Jimmy, "with my Atomic-Powered Pants-Seeking Clothespin Missiles!"

Jimmy shot the clothespins into the air and they picked up all the pants—except for Jimmy's. His pants were nowhere to be seen!

Inside the store Jimmy's pants were busy rounding up other pants. Jimmy yanked on the door, but it was locked. "Oh, no!" he cried. "My pants are outsmarting me!"

Just then Cindy ran up. "Listen, Neutron!" she demanded. "My future plans don't include living in a world ruled by pants. Do something!"

"I'm trying," said Jimmy. "I have to invent something else!" He grabbed his backpack and then dashed into Lucky Joe's Cleaners.

Five minutes later Jimmy burst out of the cleaners with a new invention: the Laundrotron!

"Okay, pants!" Jimmy yelled. "It's time for you to get pressed and eat starch!"

Using the Laundrotron, he attacked the army of pants with irons, starch, and fabric softener.

Back at home Jimmy's dad
was watching TV.
    "Look, sugar booger, Jimmy's on TV!
Neat!" he said.
    "Oh, my goodness!" Jimmy's mother gasped.
"We'd better go downtown!"

Jimmy watched his pants climb up the side of a building. "Those darn smarty pants! How can I stop them?" he wondered aloud. Then—brain blast! "That's it!" he said. "If I can make enough static electricity, I can zap my pants and they'll be powerless!"

The boys darted into Rug World where Carl and Sheen rolled out a long carpet. Jimmy made the Laundrotron run back and forth on it, building up loads of static electricity.

"It's hampertime!" Jimmy yelled. He aimed a super static-powered arm at his pants and fired, and just as he'd hoped, they fell off the building! As soon as the pants touched the ground, they stopped glowing. Then all the other pants fell and stopped glowing too.

The pants attack was finally over!

"You did it, Jimmy!" said Carl.

"Yeah, and now we get to go to the movies," Jimmy said.

"Not just yet, Jimmy," said a familiar voice. "Not till you clean up this mess!"

Jimmy stared at the piles of pants in the street. "Mo-ooom!"